Barbro Lindgren and Eva Eriksson

Perpetual Motion Machine

Douglas & McIntyre

VANCOUVER/TORONTO

Published in Canada by Douglas & McIntyre 1996
Originally published in Sweden by Eriksson & Lindgren 1995

Canadian Cataloguing in Publication Data

Lindgren, Barbro
Rosa, perpetual motion machine

Translation of: Lilla lokomotivet Rosa.
ISBN 1-55054-241-9

I. Eriksson, Eva. II. Title.

PZ7.L65852Ro 1996   J839.73'74   C95-931636-1

Printed in Italy

Rosa had arrived at last.
Was that a little engine that
charged out of the cage?
No, it was only Rosa.

BLOOMFIELD TOWNSHIP PUBLIC LIBRARY
1099 Lone Pine Road
Bloomfield Hills, Michigan 48302-2410

Rosa was small, but so strong. Her tiny wild eyes sparkled in her head. And she could easily knock any child to the ground.

She was so happy. She had to bite everyone as hard as she could. At first the children were very glad to see her. But then they were scared.

They hopped up onto the table, screaming and shouting, "Take her away! Take her away!"

Rosa grunted like a pig. She jumped like a rabbit. She turned somersaults like a monkey. The children laughed and yelled. But they wouldn't come down until their mothers said they had to.

The children's aunt was
asked to take Rosa. But
before she could say yes,
Rosa had made up her
mind. She was staying.

The first night Rosa slept in her cage. Even though she was small, she snored and hiccuped all night long.

The next morning Rosa felt happy. So she ran out and bit everyone's legs and tore holes in their trousers.

Then she attacked the chairs.

And when the chairs were all chewed up, she
decided to dig holes. She dug up all the carrots
and all the potatoes. Soon she was very dirty.
  Rosa loved being dirty.

Suddenly a strange dog, Pim, jumped out of
the woods. Rosa was excited, but Pim thought
she was just a baby. Pim growled and bared her
teeth, but Rosa didn't mind. She was having
too much fun tearing around. Pim growled
some more.

While Rosa was racing around, Pim began to dig a hole. Rosa rushed over and wanted to dig, too. But Pim wouldn't make room for Rosa. She was looking for a mouse.

Rosa decided to dig her own hole. But she soon lost interest.

There was no mouse in Pim's hole, anyway, only a toad that sat and stared. So Pim ran home. She didn't like toads. And she was tired of Rosa.

But from then on Pim allowed Rosa to come to her house every day. Pim often growled, but Rosa was as happy as a lark.

The most fun for Rosa was Pim's boy Adrian. He had just learned to walk. Pim didn't like it when Adrian climbed on her and hit her over the head with a can.

But Rosa loved Adrian. He could ride her all day if he wanted, and hit her over the head as hard as he could.

Sometimes Rosa got so excited that she had to wrestle with Adrian and knock him over. He didn't like that. The more she jumped on him, the more he screamed. And that was Rosa's favorite game of all.

Pim liked to chase rabbits. Rosa did not. While
Pim ran off, Rosa lay on the ground and waited.
Once a terrible little owl flew by. Rosa didn't like
the owl. It screeched too loudly.

Then a moose ambled by. Rosa was
frightened. She shut her eyes tight so she
wouldn't have to look at it.

A spider scuttled by under her
nose. Snap! She ate it.

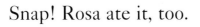

An ant scurried by
toward its nest.

Snap! Rosa ate it, too.

Pim came back. She liked Rosa now. She took
her into the garden and showed her how to pee
like a boy dog.

They fell into the deepest hole in
Pim's garden together.

Then they wrestled. Pim
always won because she was old
and Rosa was only a child.

In Pim's garden there were strawberries. Rosa ate them. There were raspberries. Rosa ate them, too. She ate everything except snails, while Pim only liked dog food from a paper bag.

Rosa's aunt thought it would do Rosa good to go for walks. But Rosa hated going for a walk. It was the worst thing in the world.

When Rosa's aunt took her out, Rosa lay on the ground. She hid under a bush. She pretended to be asleep. She wanted to go home.

Still, the next day Rosa had to go for a walk
again. She tried to growl, but only a song came out
of her mouth. She hadn't learned to growl yet. But
when she saw a woodpecker flying from tree to
tree, Rosa forgot about growling and ran after it.

Without any warning a terrible, hard cold rain
began to pour down on Rosa. It roared and
whooshed. She ran as fast as she could. And then
she was lost.

Poor little lost Rosa. People were searching for her.

Rosa's aunt called, "Rosa! Rosa!"

Had she fallen into a hole, or drowned in the pond?

"Rosa! Rosa!"
People ran through the woods calling for her.
Their clothes were soaked. But they heard
nothing. They found nothing.

They were afraid Rosa might be dead. They stopped calling. Then in the silence, from far, far away, they heard a tiny whimper.

Rosa was under a tree in the meadow. She was very wet and very, very scared. And she trembled all over.

Rosa was the happiest she
had ever been. She bit everyone
as hard as she could. Then she
spun round and round like a top.
Round and round and round
until, oops, she fell over
backward, fast asleep.